but I know she still loves me.

My mummy goes to work,
but I know she still cares about me.

My mummy goes to work,

but I know she still thinks about me all the time.

I know she'd like to be cuddling me.

I know she'd like to be tickling me.

I know she'd like to be playing games with me . . .

drawing with me . . .

bike riding with me . . .

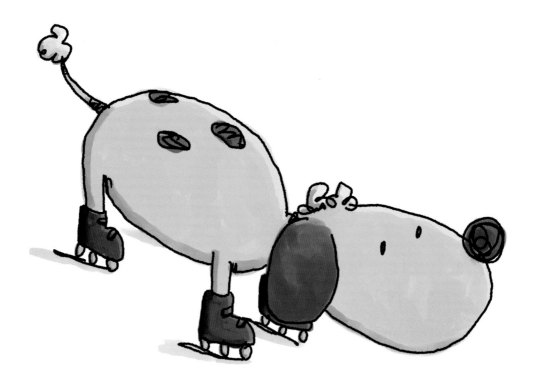

rollerblading with me . . .

painting pictures with me . . .

My mummy goes to work,
but I know she'd like
to be pushing me
on my swing.

How do I know?

Because my mummy comes home from work!

And when she does, she tells me she loves me SO MUCH . . .

tickles me SO MUCH . . .

bike rides with me SO MUCH...

rollerblades with me SO MUCH . . .

paints with me **SO MUCH** . . .

and pushes me
on my swing

SO MUCH . . .

For my wife Claire, the hardest
working mum I know K.G.

For Kendra D.M.

First published as *My Mum Goes to Work* in 2006.
This edition published in 2014.
Written by Kes Gray
Illustrated by David Milgrim

British Library Cataloguing in Publication Data.
A catalogue record of this book is available
from the British Library.

ISBN: 978 1 444 92141 0

10 9 8 7 6 5 4 3 2 1

Hodder Children's Books is a division
of Hachette Children's Books,
an Hachette UK Company,
338 Euston Road, London, NW1 3BH
www.hachette.co.uk

Printed in China.